PUFFIN BOOKS
DUSTBIN CHARLIE

Grandad calls him Dustbin Charlie because he likes to
see what people have thrown away in their dustbins.
So when the dustbins are replaced with plastic bags,
Charlie is bored. But then the builders at Number 10
get a skip for their rubbish. Soon everyone in the
neighbourhood is putting their rubbish in it too! And
in the skip, to his great delight, Charlie spots the toy
he has always longed for. But the following morning it
has gone. Someone else must have taken it out of the
skip – but who? Charlie gets a big surprise when he
discovers the culprit.

Ann Pilling was born and spent the early part of her
childhood in Warrington, in the north western
industrial area of England that forms the setting of her
novels. She taught in a local primary school, then
attended King's College, University of London,
where she gained a BA Hons. and an M.Phil. in
English. After graduating, Ann taught English in High
Wycombe. She now lives in Oxford with her family.

Other books by Ann Pilling

Ann Pilling

Dustbin Charlie

Illustrated by Jean Baylis

PUFFIN BOOKS

PUFFIN BOOKS

Published by the Penguin Group
Penguin Books Ltd, 27 Wrights Lane, London W8 5TZ, England
Penguin Books USA Inc., 375 Hudson Street, New York, New York 10014, USA
Penguin Books Australia Ltd, Ringwood, Victoria, Australia
Penguin Books Canada Ltd, 10 Alcorn Avenue, Toronto, Ontario, Canada M4V 3B2
Penguin Books (NZ) Ltd, 182–190 Wairau Road, Auckland 10, New Zealand

Penguin Books Ltd, Registered Offices: Harmondsworth, Middlesex, England

First published by Viking Kestrel 1988
Published in Puffin Books 1990
10 9 8 7 6 5 4

Text copyright © Ann Pilling, 1988
Illustrations copyright © Jean Baylis, 1988
All rights reserved

Printed in England by Clays Ltd, St Ives plc

Contents

For Valerie and Nigel

A Visit to Grandad's

His real name was "Timothy
Charles Treadwell", but
Grandad called him "Dustbin
Charlie". This was because his
very best thing was watching
the rubbish men with their
yellow lorry. They stopped at
each house, picked up the
dustbin and emptied it into a
special grinder. Then the

grinder chewed everything up with a great clanking noise. Grandad lived in a house on Union Street, and that's where this story happened.

They didn't have dustbins at Charlie's – he lived on a farm in

the country. Their house was in a long green valley with hills all round. They had two cats and three dogs, twenty hens and a hundred sheep. But there were no children to play with at all.

Spring was Mum and Dad's busiest time, because all the lambs came. Mum fed the sickly ones with a baby's bottle and Dad put the tiny ones by the cooker to keep warm. There wasn't much time to talk to Charlie and he got lonely all by himself.

10

Then Grandad phoned him up. "It's time you came to stay," he said. "Go and pack. I'm coming straight over."

Charlie ran upstairs to find
his suitcase. He was still looking
for his pyjama bottoms when
Grandad's old car rattled into
the farmyard. "Back next
week," he told Mum and Dad.

"Jump in, Charlie", and they bumped through the gate.

The bumps made a wheel cover fall off. It went spinning down the lane like a silver plate. Grandad was a bit of an inventor and he mended the car himself. But sometimes the things he mended fell to bits.

Charlie held the silver plate all the way to town. He'd still got it when they rattled into Union Street. Grandma heard the rattles and opened her front door. "Here's Charlie," shouted Grandad. "Here's Dustbin Charlie."

Grandma frowned. "He's grown-up now," she said. "I'm sure he doesn't like that baby name. Anyway, we don't have smelly dustbins any more, we have nice plastic bags." Grandma was mad on cleaning and Grandad had to do his inventions in the garden shed.

They were too messy for the house.

On dustbin morning Charlie stared glumly through the front window. Every doorstep had a neat plastic sack on it, all ready for the yellow lorry. The rubbish men had come and gone in a flash; he couldn't see all the interesting things that people had thrown away. Those

shiny black bags had changed
everything.

He pulled a face.

"What's up?" asked
Grandad.

"It's boring without
dustbins," Charlie told him.
"There's nothing to look at any
more."

Grandad scratched his chin and had a think. He'd liked the dustbins too. When Grandma wasn't looking, he'd got bits and pieces from them for his inventions.

"Keep your eyes skinned," he said. "Number 10's just been sold and the builders are starting work this week. They'll be throwing all sorts of stuff out of there."

Number 10 was the house you could see from Grandma's front room. It was very tall and very thin and it went up and up. The paint was chipped, the dirty windows were broken, and

weeds as tall as Charlie grew in
the little front garden. "Nobody
loves that house," he said.

"Yes, it's a real disgrace,"
agreed Grandma, coming in to
dust round.

But Grandad just smiled.

"You wait," he told Charlie. "You wait till those builders start work on it. It'll be as good as new soon." And he went off to his shed to mend Mrs Next Door's pop-up toaster.

It was a cold wet morning and Grandma was doing her baking. Charlie pushed a chair up to the front window, stood on it and looked out.

Outside
Number 10

The rain plonked down in
bucketfuls and nothing
happened for ages. Only three
people walked down Union
Street: Curly Harry, the tramp
who slept in the park, old Mrs
Batts, who lived at Number 23,
and Frank, the paper-boy.

Curly Harry had a plastic
carrier-bag on his head to keep

the rain off. Mrs Batts had a red
umbrella. Frank didn't have
anything at all and his wet hair
hung down like black string.

Charlie decided to go and help Grandma make cakes. He was just going through the door when he heard a noise in the street. A huge red truck had stopped outside Number 10 and some men were getting out of it.

"It's the builders," he said to
himself and he climbed on to
the chair again to see what
happened.

First they propped the front
door open with a brick. Then
the boss stood in the back of the
truck and handed things down –

hammers and shovels and bags
of cement. When everything
had been unloaded, the truck
moved off. Then they all went
inside and had cups of tea.
Charlie could see them through
the dirty windows.

The rain still sloshed down.
"No outside work today," said
the boss, looking up at the sky
from the doorway of Number

10. "We can't do much anyway, not till the skip comes", and he shut the rickety old door.

Charlie went down the garden to Grandad's shed. He was making toast on Mrs Next Door's toaster. "Have a piece," he said. "I've fixed it."

"What's a skip?" asked Charlie, munching away.

"It's a great big box, for putting rubbish in. Want some more?"

"Yes, please. Is a skip bigger than a dustbin?"

"*Much* bigger."

"Well, they're getting one for Number 10."

"Told you they'd be throwing stuff out, didn't I?" said Grandad. Then, "Oh, *heck*!" Slice of bread number 2 had stuck in the toaster and the shed was full of black smoke. "I'll have to start again with this," he said, scratching his shiny bald head.

Charlie slipped a bit of burnt toast into his pocket (it was good for drawing pictures with), then he went back to see what the builders were doing.

The big red truck had come
back with the skip. It was
lowering it on to the road outside
Number 10 with a great
clanking noise. All the men
stood round watching. So did

29

Curly Harry. The rain dripped off his carrier-bag hat and sploshed into the puddles. "Easy does it!" shouted the boss, and the skip hit the pavement with a loud boomy sound.

Charlie went up close to get a better look. It was a huge iron box, thin at the bottom and fat at the top, and it was painted banana yellow. Inside there was room for ten dustbins and twenty Charlies. That skip was nearly as big as Grandma's kitchen.

It sat there all day. The builders kept popping out of

Number 10 to throw things into
it – old floor-boards and rusty
pipes, half a cooker and a
broken-down TV. But Charlie
could only watch till dinner. In
the afternoon they all wrapped
up warm and went to visit
Auntie Alice across the park.

When they got back, the
builders had gone home, but
the shiny yellow skip was still
outside Number 10. It was piled
high with rubbish now, but
Grandad said the red truck
would be back first thing
tomorrow to empty it. Charlie

33

got worried. He wanted to have a good look at all that stuff before it disappeared.

Grandma didn't like him grubbing about in the dirt, so he sneaked out while she was running his bath. He couldn't see over the top, so he stuck his hands in the air and pulled himself up. Then he looked in.

Inside the Skip

The skip wasn't just full of builders' rubbish, there were lots of other things too. People must have come along Union Street and slipped them in while the men weren't looking. They all looked like things that were no use any more, things that should go to the dump. It was quicker using the skip though.

Under the Number 10 rubbish Charlie saw a big blue blanket with holes in. Then he saw a baby's pram with crumpled wheels. Then he saw a cracked sink with no taps.

He was just about to climb
down when he saw IT. So he
swung himself up again.

IT was lying on top of the blue blanket with its feet under some planks. It was all rusty and dented and its silver paint had been scratched right off. But it still had two arms and two legs and the wonderful smile on its face that Charlie remembered so well. It was the Walking Tin Man from the TV advert, the one that cost a year's pocket-money.

"Sorry, Charlie," Dad had said when he had wanted it for his birthday. "Toys like that cost big money, and we need some new cows." Instead, he'd had an aeroplane book and

some new jeans. They weren't nearly as good as the Walking Tin Man.

Charlie leaned right down into the skip and pulled till the Tin Man sat upright with a clonking sound. The little door in its back was open and the works were sticking out. All the

wires and springs inside were
bust. You'd have to be a genius
to mend it now. The poor old
Tin Man would never walk
again.

He still wanted it, though. It
was nearly as big as he was.
It'd look great in his bedroom.
He tugged and tugged, trying

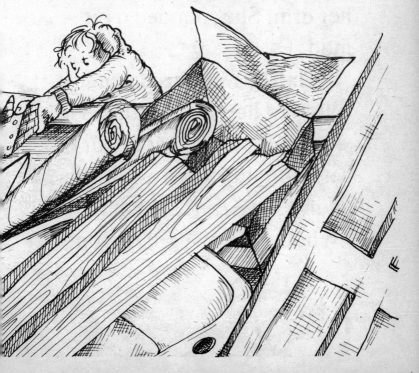

to get it out from under the planks. Then a voice across the street shouted, "Charlie? *Charlie*! What are you doing, grubbing about in that dirty old skip? I've been calling you for ten minutes, and your bath's going cold!" It was Grandma, with a fluffy striped towel over her arm. She sounded a bit mad.

Charlie went inside and followed her up the stairs. He was trying to tell her about the Tin Man, but she was rather deaf. "A *tin can*?" she said. "What on earth do you want

with an old *tin can*? There are
plenty of those in your
Grandad's shed. Now come on,
this water's getting cold."

But he thought about the
poor Tin Man all through his
bath and afterwards, when
Grandad read him a story.

Before going to sleep, he lifted
the curtains and peeped out.
The big yellow skip gleamed
gently in the light from the
street lamp, and there was

Curly Harry, poking about inside it with a stick. He was still wearing his plastic-bag hat.

Old Mrs Batts came along with her dog, Jim. She stopped by the skip too and peered over the side. Then Frank came up on his bicycle. He was on his evening round and the front basket was full of papers. He stood up on his pedals and looked at all the rubbish, then he pulled at something, but it wouldn't come out. Everyone was interested in that skip.

"It's got a Walking Man in it," Charlie said sleepily as Grandad tucked him in. But

Grandma switched the light off. "A talking *pan*? You need a good night's sleep," she said.

"Sweet dreams, Charlie," whispered Grandad.

And they were sweet. They were about him and the Tin Man, walking round the farmyard hand in hand.

The Tin Man Vanishes

Charlie overslept next morning. When he opened his eyes, he could hear the builders shouting to each other outside Number 10. Perhaps the skip had been emptied already. He pulled on his clothes and ran downstairs, three steps at a time.

Phew, what a relief! There it

was, with the planks and pipes
still sticking out of it.

When nobody was looking,
he clambered up the side again.
But he got a shock when he
looked in. The builders' rubbish

was still there, but nothing else
was. Someone must have visited
the skip in the middle of the
night.

Where was the old blue
blanket? And the pram? And
the sink with no taps?

Who could have wanted such
useless things?

Worst of all, where was the poor Tin Man? *He* wasn't useless, even though he couldn't walk. Charlie had wanted him very much indeed.

"Someone's taken things out of the skip," he said at breakfast.

"What things?" mumbled Grandad, his mouth full of cornflakes.

"An old pram and a blanket with holes and a sink with no taps. It's not fair."

"What's not fair?" said Grandma. "Who wants old junk like that?"

"It's not fair about the Tin Man."

"The *thin ham*? That's good thick bacon you're eating. Nothing thin about that," she sniffed.

But Grandad winked. "Cheer up, Charlie," he said. "It was only a load of old rubbish after all."

"The Tin Man wasn't rubbish," whispered Charlie, chewing his bacon.

Grandad wasn't listening. He said he'd got a very busy day in his garden shed.

It rained all morning and all afternoon. The builders stayed inside Number 10 with the door shut, so there was nothing much to see. Instead, Charlie helped Grandma clean out the attic.

By tea-time they'd got six
bags of rubbish lined up in the
hall, neatly fixed at the top with
wire tags. Grandma was a very
neat person. "Just ask those

builders if we can put them in that skip of theirs," she told Charlie.

So he hopped across the street and stuck his nose through Number 10's letter-box. "Please can we put

Gran's rubbish in your skip?" he shouted.

"Sure," the boss told him, coming outside. "Nothing much doing today. Too wet. That's why this is only half full. See anything you fancy? It's amazing what people throw into our skip", and he lifted Charlie right up so he could look for himself.

There was nothing inside except bricks and wire coat-hangers.

"Does your gran want these?" said the boss.

"Shouldn't think so," replied Charlie. "She found hundreds

of those in her attic. They're in
her plastic bags. You don't
know where that Tin Man went,
do you?" He'd been secretly
hoping it might have come
back.

The boss shook his head. "Haven't seen no Tin Man," he said. "There was a pram too, yesterday, and a sink, and a rotten old blanket. All gone by this morning. Can't think what people want them things for."

"If the Tin Man comes back, will you let me know?"

"Sure. Let's be having your gran's rubbish then", and the boss rolled up his sleeves.

A Walk Down Union Street

The weather cheered up after tea so they all went for a quick walk to the park. Grandad was a bit grumpy; he'd had a difficult day with his inventions.

"I could help," offered Charlie. "Let me help when we get back."

But Grandad shook his head. "There are bits and

pieces all over the place," he said. "Too many for you to sort out."

"Too many for me too," Grandma told him. "Now, if you'd just get that shed cleared out, we could grow some seeds

in it and have flowers for the
garden, like Mrs Batts."

"Mrs Batts doesn't have a
garden," Charlie pointed out.

"No, but she puts flowers in
little pots. You can put them in
anything."

"You certainly can,"
Grandad said as they walked
past Number 23. "Just look at
that!"

Charlie looked. Outside Mrs Batts's front door there was an old sink with no taps, and it was full of flowers: big round red ones at the back and bushy little blue ones at the front. White starry ones peeped out in between. It was really pretty.

"Well, I never did," said Grandma as they walked by. "Fancy using an old sink to put flowers in. But how did she get it down the street?"

"I fetched it," said a voice. "I fetched it in this", and a bicycle bell went "ting-a-ling". But the bell wasn't on a bike, it

was screwed to an old pram. Paper-boy Frank had uncrumpled the wheels and filled it with copies of the *Daily Bugle*.

"It's smashing, this pram is," he told them. "I can do my rounds quicker with this; it fits more papers. I can get back to watch *Top of the Pops* now I've got my pram", and he went off, whistling.

"Well, I never did,"
repeated Grandma as they
walked round the park. "Fancy
using an old pram for a paper
round. But how did he
uncrumple the wheels?"

"I helped," said a voice, and
they all looked down. There
was Curly Harry, stretched out
on his usual bench. He was still

wearing his plastic-bag hat and
he was all covered up with a
bright blue blanket. It had been
very neatly mended.

"Frank's mum sewed all the
holes up," he said proudly,
"and I straightened those pram

wheels for him, with me own bare hands. That's what living outdoors does for you," he told Charlie. "Gives you strength. See? I'll need this blanket when the nights get chilly. It's a bit of all right, this blanket is."

"Well, I never, never did,"
muttered Grandma as they
walked home.

"So it wasn't just a load of
old rubbish, was it?" Charlie

yawned as he snuggled into bed
that night. "The stuff in that
skip was all useful to
somebody."

"You're right, Charlie," said
Grandad. "The sink's full of

flowers, the pram's full of papers and the blanket's keeping Curly Harry warm."

"It's to be hoped he washed it," added Grandma, plumping up the pillows.

"I wonder who got the Tin Man, though," Charlie said sleepily.

"That child's still going on
about tin cans," Grandma said
to Grandad as they went down
the stairs. "I wouldn't be
surprised if he'd got a
temperature."

The Big Breakfast Mystery

In the morning it all felt very mysterious. Charlie woke up feeling hungry, but he wasn't allowed into the kitchen till Grandad said so.

Grandma was part of the mystery too. "Close your eyes!" she shouted as he came through

the door, and she tied a tea-towel round his head so he couldn't peep.

Grandad took one hand and Grandma took the other. Then

they led him across the floor
and helped him to sit at the
breakfast table. "But this isn't
my place!" shouted Charlie. He
always sat by the window, and
getting there was a bit of a
squeeze. Gran's kitchen was
quite small.

"No, there's somebody else in your place today," said Grandad, and he whipped off the tea-towel.

Charlie's eyes turned as round as marbles. Then he pinched himself in case he was dreaming. Sitting in his chair was the Walking Tin Man. The

rust had gone, so had the dents;
and that beaming smile of his
was bigger than ever. The sun
shone through the window,
making him all silvery.

"But someone took him in
the night . . ." began Charlie.
"First he was in the skip, then

he'd gone. I asked the boss at
Number 10 . . ." and he touched
the Tin Man's face, just in case
he wasn't real.

Grandad and Grandma
looked at each other; then they
looked at Charlie. They were
smiling.

"So *that's* why you spent all yesterday in the shed," he said. "You were doing an invention with the Tin Man. It was *you* who got him out of that skip!"

"Took me ages to mend him, too," grunted Grandad. "Much longer than that toaster. Come on, then."

"What do you mean 'Come on'?"

"Well, you want to see him walk, don't you?"

"Yes, but . . ." He didn't like to say any more. He knew all about Grandad's inventions. Next door's toaster was still

sticking, and some more bits
had fallen off his old car.
Charlie would be quite happy
just *looking* at the Walking Tin
Man. He was lovely now he was
all shiny.

But Grandad was very
excited. He carried Tin Man
through the front door and
stood him on the pavement.
Then he opened the flap in his
back and pressed some

switches. "Now then," he said grandly. "Stand back everybody."

Tin Man made a squeaky sound, tottered forwards, then fell flat on his face. Grandad

rushed to pick him up while the
builders at Number 10 stood
and laughed. Charlie looked at
the sky.

Grandma's clean doorstep
was soon littered with tools
from the shed. Grandad was

determined to get Tin Man walking. Curly Harry came past and stared. So did old Mrs Batts. Then Frank whizzed by with a pram full of papers. They all stopped and looked at Tin Man, lying on the pavement

with screwdrivers stuck in his back.

"What a laugh!" shouted Frank. But Charlie wasn't laughing. He felt sorry for him, all floppy in the gutter.

At last Grandad shouted, "That's it!" and pulled Tin Man on to his feet again. "Watch this," he told Charlie.

There was a grinding sort of noise and Tin Man rocked slightly. This time one foot went in front of the other and the shiny tin hands whirred up and down. Slowly at first, but gathering speed, he moved off.

A bit further up the street, paper-boy Frank called out, "Good on you, mate!" He'd just delivered the *Bugle* to Number 17.

At Number 23 Mrs Batts
clapped her hands and cheered
as Tin Man rocked by. She was
out on the pavement, watering
her sink.

Number 23 was next to the park. When he heard the funny clanking noise, Curly Harry threw off his blue blanket and got up from his bench to see what was happening.

And there he was, smiling
his silvery smile, with Charlie
and Grandad and Mrs Batts
and the builders all coming up
behind.

*That old Tin Man had walked
right down Union Street!*